Reach Incorporated | Washington, DC

Shout Mouse Press

Reach Incorporated / Shout Mouse Press
Published by
Shout Mouse Press, Inc.
www.shoutmousepress.org

Copyright © 2014 Reach Education, Inc.
ISBN-13: 978-0692300787 (Shout Mouse Press, Inc.)
ISBN-10: 0692300783

All rights reserved. No part of this book may be reproduced or transmitted in any form
or by any means, electronic or mechanical, including photocopying, recording, or by an
information storage and retrieval system, without written permission from the
publisher, excepting brief quotes used in reviews.

This is for everyone,
because we can all be courageous.

Every day after school in the back of Reach Middle School,

kids play basketball.

A three-on-three pick-up game is just finishing up. Da'Monte fakes right and one of his teammates sets a pick. Da'Monte hits a game-winning three-pointer.

His friend Jasmine runs up to him and is the first one to say, "Congrats on the win!"

"Thanks," Da'Monte says. "Meet me by the playground so we can walk to my Gran's house. I have to pick up my shoes for gym class tomorrow."

Da'Monte's teammates interrupt by picking him up in the air and saying, "Good game!"

Jasmine waves at Da'Monte and leaves the gym.

Marco, the center from the losing team, walks over to Da'Monte. "You guys won by luck. Your team is still losers," he says.

Da'Monte starts to shake his head, like he knows it's not true, but then he just shrugs his shoulders and walks towards the locker room.

After changing his clothes, Da'Monte grabs a drink of water
from the fountain in the hallway. He looks out the window.
Outside, Da'Monte can see his friend Jasmine
waiting for him by the swings.

He sees Marco and his sidekicks making their way towards Jasmine. Marco is always teasing kids. Especially kids who are having a rough time in school. Jasmine is an easy target because she is an outcast and doesn't have a lot of friends. Kids think that Jasmine is weird because she wears shirts that nobody thinks are funny, like her "Meatballs" shirt. Who wears shirts that say "Meatballs" anyway?

Da'Monte likes Jasmine because she is unique. He likes her style. She's goofy, you know? She can express her feelings without worrying about kids judging her.

But he knows if he goes outside to defend her, Marco will pick on him. He'll say that Da'Monte likes Jasmine, and he doesn't want that getting around school. So instead of going to help, Da'Monte just stands there and watches.

Marco and his sidekicks walk up to Jasmine and point at her shirt and start laughing. Marco wraps his arms around his body like he is cold or hugging himself and makes kissy faces at her.

Da'Monte can tell that Jasmine is crying. She begins to run away from the boys.

Da'Monte runs out of the school to catch up to Jasmine.

"Jasmine, wait."

She turns around with tears in her eyes.

"I saw what happened," he says. "Are you okay?"

Jasmine says, "If you saw what happened, why didn't you help?" She begins to run again and yells back at him: "You just watched me get bullied! You're just like everybody else, standing on the sidelines."

Da'Monte walks slowly with his head down to his grandmother's house, which is just across the street. She's standing on her front porch when he arrives.

"**H**ey Grandma."

"Hi, Da'Monte. I saw Jasmine running off crying from the playground. Is she okay?"
Da'Monte sighs. "Some boys were bullying her after the basketball game."
"So, why didn't you help?" his grandmother asks.
"I didn't want to get bullied, too," he answers.

His grandmother shakes her head. "I'm disappointed. You should have helped your friend. You shouldn't always just think about yourself." She gets up and says, "I have something for you. I was in the same position you were in when I was your age."

"You were MY age?" Da'Monte says. "Man, that was a LONG time ago."
His grandmother chuckles and says, "Hold on."

She walks up the stairs, and when she returns, she's holding a big blue hoodie.

"Here. This is my hoodie from junior high," she says.
"What can a hoodie do for me?" Da'Monte asks. "Protect me from the cold and the rain?"
"Trust me. It can help you a lot, like it did for me."

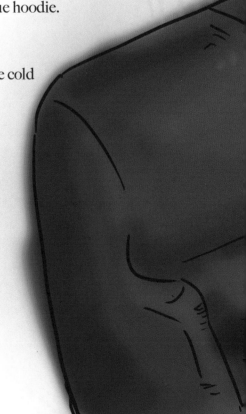

Da'Monte takes the hoodie home to see what it can do.

When he gets there he quickly says hello to his parents and runs upstairs to his bedroom. Da'Monte takes the hoodie out of his backpack and lays it down on his bed. He wonders, *What's so special about this hoodie that Gran thinks it will help me? It's just a regular ol' hoodie.*

Da'Monte closes his bedroom door and tries it on.

He looks in the mirror. It's so big that the hood covers half his face. He can only see his nose and mouth.

He thinks to himself, *This hoodie doesn't work. I thought it was going to give me power.*

The next morning, Da'Monte arrives at school and sees his friend, William.

Da'Monte asks, "Are you going to play basketball with us after school?"
"Sure, I don't have anything better to do," William answers. "What's that in your book bag?"
"It's a hoodie my Gran gave me."
"A hoodie your Gran gave you?" William laughs. "Ok, then, let me see. Put it on."

Da'Monte takes the hoodie out of his book bag and puts it on. The hood hangs over his face, hiding his eyes.

"It looks good. But that's a fat-daddy hoodie," William says.

They both laugh.

Marco walks up to the lockers and says, "Hey Wheelie."
"That's not my name," says William.
"Well, you're in a wheelchair so I can call you 'Wheelie,'" says Marco.

"Marco, stop," says Da'Monte. "Why are you messing with William?"
Marco looks confused. "Who are you? Do you even go to this school?" he asks.
Da'Monte can't believe it. He doesn't' recognize him with the hoodie covering his face!

"I do go to this school, but you will never know who I am," Da'Monte answers.
Marco backs off and says, "Okay, whatever. Later, Wheelie."
He walks away, banging lockers as he walks.

The hallways clear and students start making their way to class.

Da'Monte runs to the bathroom and looks at himself in the mirror. He thinks, *What just happened? It couldn't have been me. It had to be the hoodie. Could Gran possibly be right?*

Da'Monte takes the hoodie back off and holds it in his hands. He says to himself, "Marco doesn't know who I am, but I do." He puts the hoodie back in his book bag and heads to class.

During the school day, Marco tries to bully a few kids. He tries to smack books out of a kid's arms, but Da'Monte is there to stop him. He tries to take a boy's lunch money, but Da'Monte is there once again. One time, he sticks his foot out to trip a girl, but Da'Monte catches her in the last moment.

By the end of the day, kids around school are talking about the bully-stopper in the fat-daddy hoodie. *Who is that guy?* they want to know.

Finally the bell rings and the school day is over. Da'Monte gets his book bag from his locker. He thinks about Jasmine and how he can earn her friendship back. While he's thinking, he overhears her voice echoing up the stairwell: "Stop making fun of my hair!"

Da'Monte goes down the stairs and hears Marco say, "Ok, piggy head!"

Da'Monte stops in the stairwell and grabs his hoodie out of his book bag. He puts it on and runs down the rest of the stairs.

Da'Monte sees Marco and his sidekicks surrounding Jasmine.

He says, "Marco why are you always being a bully?" "Because I can 'bully' whoever I want to," Marco replies.

Jasmine steps back and stands next to Da'Monte.
Da'Monte says, "Not in this school. I'm here to stop you."
Marco just shakes his head and says, "Just wait, I'll get you next time."
He walks away with his sidekicks.

Jasmine turns to Da'Monte and says,
"What's your name? You sound like an old friend of mine, but you couldn't be him because he never stood up for me."

Da'Monte pauses and says, "You're welcome...
Maybe I—I mean 'your friend'—didn't have the confidence to stand up for you. Anyway. I have to go now. See you around."
"Sure," Jasmine replies.

Da'Monte walks away and heads towards the school gym, feeling amazed that Jasmine doesn't recognize him, but wishing that she did.

Da'Monte enters the gym.

He sees Jasmine and William talking on the other side of the court and starts heading their way, but Marco stops him.

"What are you still doing here? Didn't I tell you to get lost?" Marco asks.
"I go to school here," Da'Monte replies.
"No, you don't," Marco says.

Da'Monte is confused at first, but then he realizes that he still has his hoodie on. He thinks to himself, *What do I do now?*

A crowd of students starts to surround Marco and Da'Monte.

A kid from the crowd yells, "Who are you in that fat-daddy hoodie?"

Another kid says, "Are you trying to be a superhero?"

Da'Monte doesn't know what to do.

The hoodie was his protection. If he takes it off, will people still take him seriously? He's just Da'Monte, definitely no superhero. Will they start to make fun of him, too?

Da'Monte looks over at Jasmine in the crowd. She is looking right at him. He thinks, *I'm going to do this for Jasmine.*

Da'Monte slowly takes his hoodie off.

He pulls it over his head and throws it on the gym floor.

"I don't need a hoodie to speak my mind or to stand up for other people," he says.

Marco says in surprise, "Da'Monte?!" Then quickly he adds, "You're still a loser."

"If I'm a loser, then why am I always stopping you, and why are you always picking on people who can't stand up for themselves?" Da'Monte asks.

Jasmine steps out of the crowd and says, "Marco, man, you are the true loser."

William agrees and says, "You bully kids for no reason."

The crowd gathers around Da'Monte and cheers, "Yeah, Marco, you're the loser!"

They start chanting in a sing-song way that echoes off the walls.

Marco throws his hands in the air and walks away. He waves some of his sidekicks over, but nobody moves. Marco is left alone on the sidelines, and he punches the wall. The other kids laugh.

When the crowd loses interest, Da'Monte walks over to him and asks, "How does it feel to be a loser?"

Marco is like, "Whatever." But he almost looks like he might cry. Da'Monte is shocked—he didn't think that was possible. In some ways it feels good, but in other ways he doesn't want to be just another bully.

Da'Monte says, "Man, forget it. Just leave kids alone. And come watch me sink another three in your face." He pushes him on the arm and fakes a jumpshot over his head. *Swishhhhh.*

Da'Monte, Marco, and their friends begin another three-on-three game. Marco still taunts them all, but nobody's scared of him anymore, so he quiets down.

Da'Monte is on fire on the court. He's spinning and slashing towards the basket and everything feels just right. William assists him for a jump shot from the corner, and he yells "YES!" when it goes in.

After the game, Jasmine walks up to Da'Monte and says, "I knew it was you."

"You knew?" he says. "Then why didn't you say so?"

"And mess with the fat-daddy-hoodie mystery? I'm not going to ruin their fun."

She laughs and Da'Monte laughs with her.

"I guess I'll give the hoodie back to Gran now. I think its work is done."

"Or we could give it to someone who needs it," Jasmine says. "You know, someone who tries so hard to be cool that he forgets who he is?" She punches Da'Monte lightly on the arm.

"Right, I don't know anyone like that," Da'Monte says with a grin.

Jasmine smiles back and drapes the hoodie over her back like a cape.

"Yeah, me neither."

THE END

Acknowledgements

In July 2014, twelve students embarked on an exciting journey. Tasked with the challenge of creating original children's books that reflected the diversity and reality of their world, these young people brainstormed ideas, generated potential plots, wrote, revised, and provided critiques. In the end, they created four amazing books, showing again what teenagers can do when their potential is unleashed with purpose. Our twelve authors have our immense gratitude and respect: Kyare, Za'Metria, Litzi, Makayla, Darrin, Marc, Darne'sha, Zorita, Karta, Ashley, Rico, and Daequan.

These books are a joint project between Reach Incorporated and Shout Mouse Press, and we are grateful for the leadership provided by members of both teams. From Reach, Leigh Creighton and Jeremiah Headen acted as all-important story scribes, working closely with authors to capture and develop their ideas. We simply wouldn't have been able to do it without our incredible Summer Program Director, Jusna Perrin.

From the Shout Mouse Press team, we thank Alison Klein and Annie Rosenthal for their guidance as story scribes, and Lucia Liu and Mira Ko for their beautiful illustrations. Kathy Crutcher served as story coach and series editor. We are grateful for the time and talents of these writers and artists!

Most of all, we thank those of you who have purchased the books. It is your support that allows us to support teen authors in engaging young readers. We hope the smiles created as you read match those expressed as we wrote.

-- Mark Hecker
Reach Incorporated, Founder and Executive Director

About the Authors

Ashley Cooper is sixteen years old and attends Ballou Senior High School in Washington, DC. She is loving and supportive but also serious at times. Ashley is the youngest of six kids, and on her dad's side she is the middle child of five. She is very passionate about drawing and singing, and she is a very good athlete. This is her first children's book.

Daequan Golden was a Reach tutor at Perry Street Prep in Washington, DC. He never leaves the house without picking his hair. Daequan loves to play basketball, and he loves shoes. Daequan also loves his hair. This is his first book.

About the Authors

Rico McCard goes to Eastern High School in Washington, DC, and is in the eleventh grade. This is his second children's book. His first book was *Trio Plus One*, published in 2013. Rico likes to play basketball and baseball, and he is a Lead Tutor with Reach Incorporated.

About the Illustrator

Lucia Liu is a Painting & Printmaking major at Virginia Commonwealth University. She creates paintings, screenprints, etchings, lithographs, and illustrations and has exhibited in numerous shows in the Richmond area. In addition to art, she is a longtime participant in various musical ensembles as a violinist, and enjoys playing guitar and writing creatively in her free time. Her previous illustration credits include *One Lonely Camel* and *Trio Plus One*. See more of her work here: http://cargocollective.com/lucialiu

About Reach Incorporated

Reach Incorporated develops confident grade-level readers and capable leaders by training teens to teach younger students, creating academic benefit for all involved.

Founded in 2009, Reach recruits high school students to be elementary school reading tutors. Elementary school students average 1.5 grade levels of reading growth per year of participation. This growth – equal to that created by highly effective teachers – is created by high school students who average more than two grade levels of growth per year of program participation.

As skilled reading tutors, our teens noticed that the books they read with their students did not reflect their reality. At Reach, we trust teens with real responsibility for things that matter to them. So, when confronted with this challenge, we did what seemed most appropriate: we had our teens write new books. Through fanciful stories with diverse characters, our books invite young readers to explore the world through words.

By purchasing our books, you support student-led, community-driven efforts to improve educational outcomes in the District of Columbia.

Learn more about all our books at www.reachincorporated.org/books.

About Shout Mouse Press

Shout Mouse Press is a publishing house for unheard voices.

- We promote diversity in literature by empowering under-represented communities worldwide to develop and write their stories, and then we professionally publish them for a broad audience.
- We create tangible, marketable products for the nonprofits and communities we serve in order to amplify, diversify, and innovate their outreach and fundraising.

The founding of Shout Mouse Press was inspired by a collaboration with Reach Incorporated during the summer of 2013 when we helped their teen tutors produce their first set of original children's books. We witnessed the way those books expanded the horizons of possibility for both their authors and readers alike, and that emboldened us to bring the power of publication to more communities whose voices need to be heard. We now partner with nonprofit organizations serving communities in need and design book projects that help further their missions. Shout Mouse authors have produced original children's books, memoir collections, and novels-in-stories. Learn more at ShoutMousePress.org.

JUL 0 7 2015